Are You a Nutjob?

Poetic Observations On a Trump Presidency

James Sawers

Are You a Nutjob?

Books of poetry by James Sawers

Nothing Series:

Nothing Works 2nd ED
Meditations on Aikido, Buddhism,
the Tao, Zen, and other
inconsequential things...

Nothing Special: Vol II
Nothing Matters: Vol III
Nothing Exists; Vol IV
Nothing Flows Vol. V

War Series:

Words of War
Warm Beer Is Not Cool
Go Tell the Crows

Color Series:

Red
Lust Is a Monster
Poems of Life, Love, and Loss

Green
The Other Monster

Blue
The Indigo Moments of Life

Trumpets
Poetic Observations
on a Presidency

Are You a Nutjob?
Poetic Observations On
a Trump Presidency

Life Series

In the Shadows of the Ordinary
Too Deep For Tears
Rainy Nights in Chicago
Silent Love
She Wears the Wind
Accidental Gods

Religion/Mysticism

War of Swords
Poems on Religion,
Mysticism, & a Touch
of Science

Politics

Are You a Nutjob?

Nothing-Werks, Inc.
(Where Nothing Matters)
nothingwerks42@gmail.com

Are You a Nutjob?
*Poetic Observations
On a Trump Presidency*

Copyright (C) 2019 James Sawers
ALL RIGHTS RESERVED

While the material in this book is copyrighted,
excerpts of this book may be reproduced or
transmitted in any form or by any means, electronic
or mechanical, including photocopying, recording or
by any information storage and retrieval system,
as long as attribution is given to the author.

First Printing – February 2019
ISBN: 9781797433660

Are You a Nutjob?

The weakest link in any society is us.
~ Rachel Botsman

Are You a Nutjob?

Overview

This book represents the second volume in the ever disturbing Trump Presidency saga. It is mostly a book of poetry, with a couple of very short essays thrown in, inspired, mostly, by Trump's very own words and actions.

Whatever your political bent, I think it can be stated, and agreed upon, that the candidacy and the past years of this Presidency are beyond the norm. Some would consider this a good thing, with the Washingtonian power structure shaken up and politics as usual, demolished.

Others would see the same Trump behaviors as not only beyond the norm, but beyond the pale. This work explores this opinion and viewpoint, sometimes in a humorous way, at other times, in a more serious tone.

Make no mistake, however, whatever your political leanings, the Trump Presidency will set and affect the tone and standard of politics for years to come, and not in a good way.

With the normalization of lying and hate speech, and their promulgation, and a flat refusal to make decisions based on anything close to an evidence-based, fact-based process, the American way of life is in jeopardy. While bad behavior can sometimes be "good" political behavior, it is still bad behavior, and creates (intentional) distractions from real- time American domestic and world issues that truly need to be addressed and solved.

Not to be too melodramatic, but the world and history is watching and taking measure as Trump America puts a tremendous strain on our Constitutional, political, social, and environmental fabric. The reverberations will continue to ripple through time, even after Trump is long gone.

I sincerely hope that we all survive it.

Are You a Nutjob?

Are You a Nutjob?

I would give myself an A+.
~ Donald J. Trump

The heights of popularity and patriotism are still the beaten road to power and tyranny.
~ David Hume

A malignant megalomaniac facing no countervailing power will continue to expand his terrain until he is stopped.
~ Robert Reich

A fake emergency is much better than a real Congressional hearing.
~ Tristan Graeme Ash

For someone like Trump, global institutions, even ones that the U.S. helped to create, dilute his power, or the power he eventually hopes to garner for himself.
~ Lucy Nalangu

The Stone Age didn't end because of a shortage of stones.
~ One OPEC oil minister observed

Donald Trump is worse than any horror story I've written.
~ Stephen King

Bad behavior is almost always good politics.
~ Bruce Bueno de Mesquita

Make America Great Again.
~ Donald J. Trump

Are You a Nutjob?

Are You a Nutjob?

Contents

America 1

Humpty Dumpty 2

Shutdown! 3

Executive Time 4

Doomsday 5

Warning 7

My Gut Knows 8

La Grande Muraille 9

A Rolling Stone 10

Seems Fair 11

Lies 12

Code-Talkers 13

Spartacus! 14

Are You a Nutjob?

I Can See Russia 16

Space Force! 17

Boofing 18

Let It Rain 19

Idiotology 20

Whale? 22

Deplorables 24

Ad Astra 25

Qualifications 27

Mars Calling 28

Base Impulses 29

Rope & Guillotine 30

Enemy of the People 31

Stable Genius 32

Buttons & Bannon 33

Asteroid of Awfulness! 34

Are You a Nutjob?

The Wall	35
Duty & History	36
Toilets	37
38 Minutes at Mar-a-Lago	39
Sorry!	40
Rape	41
Parade	44
Independence Day	45
Seven Words	47
Jim Crow	48
Make the Planet Great, Again!	49
Amoral Familists	50
BBC Mars	51
Lodestar	52
Stoneman	53
Most Dangerous?	54

Politicians	56
Great People!	57
Booze, Women, & Movies	58
How Soon?	59
Choice & State	60
Concubine of Truth	63
Good-News Story	64
Predator	65
The Summit	66
Troops to the Border!	67
What to Do?	68
Women's March	69
NEWS! NEWS! NEWS!	70
Making Sense?	71
Climate Change	73
Voice of America!	74

Mr. Cohen 75

Impeachment Party 76

Summit Two 77

Some People 82

Are You a Nutjob? 86

Are You a Nutjob?

Are you a Nutjob?

America

Trump requested a *Van Gogh*
To hang in the White House
The Guggenheim suggested
Something perhaps more apropos
Something like the *America*

After all, it is covered in gold
A substance he covets
Above all else
And it is a fully functional
Golden toilet

Unlike the current America
He is supposed to be governing

Are You a Nutjob?

Humpty Dumpty

There was a crooked man...

Humpty Dumpty sat on great Wall
Humpty Dumpty had a great fall
Roses are red, violets are blue
Indictments are coming
Does that scare you?
A-tisket, a-tasket
A little White House basket
In it I put a letter to the Union
As per our very own Constitution
But all is closed and in confusion
I love a little pussy
Her coat is so very warm
And if I don't get caught
I don't have to pay her a lot
I'm scared of twelve good people, O
Green grows the Ruskies, O
Green grow the Ruskies, O
The sweetest hours I ever spent
Were spent among the Ruskies, O
Donny, Donny, pudding and hamberders pie
Kissed all the hookers and made them cry
Hickory, dickory, dock
Donny is running out of clock
Sticks and stones may break bones
But jail time will never get me
Pardon me! Pardon me!...We'll wait and see
This is the House that Donny built
Hush little Donny, don't say a word
But that is next to impossible
And so very much comical
When you ride the Tweeter-Bird
Eeny, meeny, miny moe
It is time for little Donny to go

...There was a crooked man

Shutdown!

Huston, we have a problem!
All systems have shutdown
Huston, can you hear me?
Hello, Huston, do you copy?
Damn! Hey, guys, you still open?
Hey, I know we all have problems
Including budget ones
But, we are bleeding air up here!
Temperature is dropping
And Sergei is turning blue!
Huston, you copy? Huston?
Damn, hey guys, I'm gonna try
And call China or Russia
Or, Mexico
I think they are still open!

Executive Time

Sir, what are you doing?
Executive time
I'm eating Hamberders
Executive time
I'm playing golf
Executive time
I'm taking a nap
Executive time
I watching Fox News
Executive time
I'm pouting
Executive time
I'm watching Rome burn
Executive time

Doomsday

30 seconds
30 seconds closer to doomsday!
Nuclear risks, unchecked climate change
The Doomsday Clock has been set forward
Not since the height of the Cold War
Has it been set so close to midnight
The midnight of all our souls
Of course, since this new
Setting was posted by the
Bulletin of the Atomic Scientists
We know it can't be true!
It deals with science, after all
And we all know about their
Hidden, progressive agenda
Especially by pointing out
That decline in U.S. leadership
Is a possible cause....
Those provocative statements to
An unstable nuclear power dictator
The general ant-science attitude
Just when science is needed the most
An apocalypse is closer than ever
But, what-the-hell, it's just a
Liberal, progressive, propaganda
A bunch of scientists, plus
15 Noble Laureates just don't get it!
Tick-tock, tick-tock, tick-tock
Two minutes left...
Tick-tock, tick-tock, tick-tock

Are You a Nutjob?

Citing growing nuclear risks and unchecked climate dangers, the Doomsday Clock — the symbolic point of annihilation — is now two minutes to midnight, the closest the Clock has been since 1953 at the height of the Cold War, according to a statement today (Jan. 25, 2018) by the Bulletin of the Atomic Scientists.

"In 2017, world leaders failed to respond effectively to the looming threats of nuclear war and climate change, making the world security situation more dangerous than it was a year ago — and as dangerous as it has been since World War II," according to the Atomic Scientists' Science and Security Board in consultation with the Board of Sponsors, which includes 15 Nobel Laureates.

Warning

They say poetry
Can be a warning
A record of things past
A harbinger of things to come
So, I write these words
Over your wet, wet corpse
Covered not in flowers
But in dirt and mud
And....stuff

A noble death?
I think not
Worthwhile?
I think not
So, what am I saying?
What is my meaning?
I look into the eyes
Of my fellow soldiers
And see acceptance, rage, grief

My warning?
Someday those eyes
Will be turned towards home
Towards our political leaders
And, they will accept only truth

My Gut Knows

My gut knows
It just knows
Certainly it is big enough
But it knows stuff
You have no idea how much it knows
It knows stuff even the generals don't
It knows stuff even the scientist don't
It just knows
It knows stuff I can't even tell you
It just knows
Trust me on this
I don't need to listen to trained,
Educated, brilliant leaders in their fields
My gut knows better
I bet my gut could've landed
That new probe on Mars!
Bet ya
After all, Mars just hangs there
In the night sky
How hard can it be!?
Climate change, Economics,
Military Science, Ecology,
Sociology, Education…
Who needs experts in these fields
When you have my massive gut!?
Tell me that!
Trust me
Trust my gut!

La Grande Muraille

For years I tried to teach
My dog how to speak French
With absolutely no luck
Some things just can't be done
La Grande Muraille
The Great Wall
Nope
Even in English
It doesn't make much sense!

A Rolling Stone

A rolling stone gathers no moss
But it does gather some corrupt Republicans
A rolling stone gathers no moss
But it does gather some indictments
A rolling stone gathers no moss
But it somehow gathered a Russian accent
A rolling stone gathers no moss
But a rolling stone has finally come to rest
Nestled in the shadow of Nixon

Seems Fair

Low gas prices
Arms sales
One murdered American journalist
(A fake news one, anyway)
Well, that seems like a fair trade
How can anyone criticize me?
I am saving American jobs!
I am boosting the American economy!
And, oh yeah, my properties in Saudi Arabia
Are doing quite well, too, thank you....
I'm making America great again!
Seems fair

Lies

All my lies are good lies
I'm honest about my lies
I'm telling you the truth
I lie a lot
But they are all for
The good of the country!

Would I lie?
Of course I would
But not now
This is not a lie
Would I lie?

I can say unequivocally
That all Trumps are liars!
Hey, wait a minute
If I say that, then
I'm telling the truth
Damn, I'm confused...

Code-Talkers

He called her *Pocahontas*
For him a pejorative
And taken as such
By the very men
He was supposed to be there
To honor – to honor!

The surviving Code-Talkers
From World War II
Men who had sacrificed
Men who had put their lives
Their lives on the line
For a country that now dishonored
Them in the words and actions
Of the President of the United States

That he would use such a sacred
Occasion to try and slam
A senator he was opposed to
By denigrating her ancestry
And theirs!

I wonder if the Code-Talkers
Have created a code word for him?
Could be, but what word would fit?

Spartacus!

The coffee shop was crowded
Mostly solitary people sitting
Hunched in their seats
Many still wearing winter coats
To ward off the chill
The large windows fogged over
And dripping with condensation

Outside a major snow storm
Traffic gnarled, and slow, slow
Somehow it didn't feel like Christmas
But it was – Christmas Eve in fact
Still, the coffee was hot
The wind, snow, and cold were *outside*
And I was dry and comfortable, *inside*
With all my books

So, when Santa walked through the door
Dragging with him a swirl of cold snow
I was really surprised, surprised!
He was taller than I expected
And behind him, instead of a bag of presents
He pulled a train of bedraggled people
Refugees! – I knew it as soon as I saw them!

Damn, I guess if anyone has the clout
To bring in refugees to this country
It would be Santa Claus
Or, perhaps he just bypassed everything
A *Santa Sans Frontières!*

Everyone stopped and stared
Seats were made available
Winter coats were taken off and given
Food and coffee were provided – free
Tears and thanks were offered –
By all the coffee shop customers!

Are You a Nutjob?

Now it felt like Christmas!
But, Santa had to leave
He had many more trips to make!
Remember! Remember! He cried
On the way out
WE ARE ALL SPARTACUS!
HUH! Not quite what I was expecting
But we all understood his meaning!
Merry Christmas!

I Can See Russia

On a clear day
I can see Russia
Not from across some
Cold Bering Strait
But, from my very own warm
Overly decorated penthouse!

I can also see Russia
When I visit my
Colleagues at work
(Psst...That "R" after their
Names stands for "Russia")

I can see Russia when
I look at the daily headlines
I can see Russia from
Atop my battlements -
Looking inward

I can see Russia
In my lawyer's eyes
I can see Russia
When I look into the mirror

Space Force!

Space Force
All the jokes come to mind
Space Force
Buck Rogers
Flash Gordon
The Lensmen
Hell, Starship Troopers

But, mostly I think of
Lost in Space
And Dr. Smith bumbling
His scheming way across the stars

Space Force
Starfleet Academy - I don't think so
More like Spaceballs Academy
Created to keep out the Space-Mexicans

Ad Astra – I don't think so
More like control of low-Earth orbit
So we can get a magnificent view
Of all our internment camps
And the great walls surrounding
All our borders

Space Force!
Now all we need is
The Rebel Alliance

Boofing

Boofing, Boofing, Boofing, Boofing,
Boofing, Boofing, Boofing, Boofing
Boofing, Boofing, Boofing, Boofing
Boofing, Boofing, Boofing, Boofing
Remember to go to the
Voting boof!

Boofing is slang for anal sex. The term can also be used to refer to the practice of putting alcohol or drugs up one's butt to get intoxicated

Let It Rain

Let it rain
Let the rain slide off my poncho
Let the rain dribble into my food
Let my already lukewarm coffee
In my canteen cup
Get more cold and diluted
Let my trench fill with filthy water
And my boots and feet suffer
Let my weapons and equipment
Feel slick and cold and get coated in mud
Let the rain blind me and my comrades
As bullets and bombs fly
Flaying our positions and bodies
Let the rain pour down
On our wet tombstones
Rivulets of wetness
Running over our names and graves
Let the rain come down
Let the rain fall on our world leaders
Standing in mute honor and respect
Over ceremonies and mourning
And umbrellas
Let it rain
We don't really care anymore
About the rain
But, apparently, someone does

Idiotology

He spoke and spoke
Speech after speech
Tweet after tweet

The narrow minded,
The ignorant, the stupid
The bigots, the crazoids
All ate it up, and begged for more

In large parts of the world
The pendulum has swung right
Far right

Historical forces?
As natural and predictable
As gravity, as thermodynamics?
Or, a sign of something else?

Are we approaching something new?
A new science or academic field? -
Idiotology, some call it

All the talking heads - talk
Wise ones pontificate
Comedians make jokes
Some just cry and cry

Like many, I sit and watch in shock
I see progressive global systems
Weakened, if not outright destroyed

Survivalists check their guns
And their ammo supplies
But, now, so do liberals
What can be done?

Are You a Nutjob?

We can fight and fight back
Using our systems and institutions
To protect our nation and world

Will it be enough? What happens
When a democratic system
Elects a non-democratic elite?
Not all civilizations survive

Seemingly contradictory
Many die at the height of their power
When their footprint impacts the most

So, I watch the new field of *Idiotology*
I watch it try to grasp and understand
That which appears to be non-rational
Perhaps a new psychopathology

Is on the rise, or an old one
Thriving on new fertile soil
But, I try to take the long-view

Perhaps the new field
Of *Idiotology* can help us survive
This perhaps existential threat
But, I also check my own gun

And my ammo supply
And keep my passport
And go-bag at the ready

But, there is no real escape
We are a planet-spanning culture
Connected and inter-connected
Subject to everyone's idiots

Whale?

Does it have to be a whale?
So goes the famous question
Yes, it does!

A fact is a fact
A truth is a truth
Passing a law to negate a fact
Is just sheer idiocy

Saying something is wrong
Just because it makes you look bad
Won't change the underlying facts

Does it have to be a whale?
Yes, if that's what it is

Are You a Nutjob?

You Need Science

Mr. President
Dear Republican Party
Interested Trump supporters
To all those anti-science people
Those that think science is
Some kind of left-wing conspiracy
Take heed
Yes, take heed...

Keep in mind, if you can
That you are living in your
Air-conditioned homes
Driving your late-model cars
Using your smart phones
And yelling loudly on the internet
All because of science
And, oh yes, also firing your
Modern firearms, as well!
Those nuclear weapons Trump
Is so fond of, too
Yes, all because of science

So, while you decry science
And all it has accomplished
This you might understand:
You need science to kill people!
Though, I guess, you could go back
To the basic club and knife
A large rock would do well, too...

But, I don't think you will
Willingly give up science
If that means you can't kill *en mass*
Science calls this *cognitive dissonance*
A lot of lay people just call it stupidity
Or, even more extreme, a form of insanity
But, I guess, it would take a scientist
To figure it all out

Deplorables

Being dumb is not necessarily a handicap
In fact, many seem to thrive on this

They rant and rave
Carry Tiki torches
Scream about how they are maligned
Scream about their losing their rights
Scream that they should come first
Scream about others holding them back
Scream about others taking their place
Many times, they just scream
SCREAM!

Some call them patriots
Some call them idiots and assholes
Some call them Deplorables
Some call them other things
What do you call them?

Ad Astra

I ride the trains
Rumbling and arcing
Through the city
Hearing the roar of the people
In the tracks

I ride the highways
Clogged with traffic and hostility
Parking lots full of people
Hemmed in and congested
People barely restraining
Themselves in their frustrations

Before, sometimes, people would vent
But in these days of concealed carry
People just bottle it up
The news feeds feed their paranoia
Old institutions are no longer believed
Or, fully trusted anymore
The rich get richer, and the poor....
Well, you know how that ends

Before, politicians were considered
Devious, even slimy, perhaps
But now, they just downright lie
To our very faces
These, our elected officials!

Social media seems hell bent on
Rushing us faster and faster
To the ever approaching edge
The Doomsday Clock ticks faster
And people make jokes or just
Simply do not understand

Are You a Nutjob?

Ad Astra now seems a lost dream
As AI looms on the horizon
Humans seem to get more stupid
The few bright lights getting drowned
In the ever expanding dark
Species, as a whole, have a limited lifespan
But, we may be the first to commit suicide!

Are You a Nutjob?

Qualifications

*Excuse me sir,
but what did you say
your qualifications to be
a Supreme Court Justice are?*

*Ah, you like beer.
Did I hear you correctly, sir?*

Anything else sir?

Ah, you like beer a lot.

*Thank you sir for your
frank and honest answers.*

*And, for the record, as
the nominee appears too
humble to mention it, but
he also is quite proficient
in boofing.*

*I think that wraps it up gentlemen.
Are we all now ready to vote?*

Mars Calling

Mars Calling
Hi, Houston, Mission Control
We got a message
That President Trump called
So, if you wanna patch him through
We can certainly try and talk
But does he understand that
We are not only in a very, very
Different time zone here
But, also that we are about
Twenty minutes away by radio -
One-way…!
So, conversation will be difficult
But, go ahead
I'm sure the President wouldn't
Be calling Mars Station
Unless it was really important!
But, if it's about the Pyramid of Mars
Or, the Face of Mars
Or, the Canals of Mars
Or, to get a signed picture
Of Dejah Thoris
Please, please, tell him, again
That they are not real!

Base Impulses

Even if deep down
Or, perhaps not so deep down
You tend to agree with Trump
About what he said about *shithole countries*
You must understand that
The very nature of being
Considered part of a civilized culture
Is that you try to overcome
Your base impulses – which we all have
In order to promote
The public good for all, including yourself
And that this is not just an altruistic idea
But totally a self-serving one as well

Are You a Nutjob?

Rope & Guillotine

The rope and the guillotine
Are rarely used today
But the people have long memories
And well remember that poor advice:
Let them eat cake...

Enemy of the People

Enemy of the people
The Free Press -
Yes they are!
They create division and distrust
They cause war
They are also dangerous and sick
They truly are
The enemy of the people!
If only there was some true
Reliable method of getting
My message across, my agenda
To the people, the masses
I know, I need a State run media
Where only my truth, sorry, THE truth
Will be portrayed and told
Yes, a State Fox News, for example
Hmm, just gotta do something
About that pesky 1st Amendment

Stable Genius

OMG!
I'm not just a genius!
I'm a stable genius!
And, like, I'm really smart, too!

Are You a Nutjob?

Buttons & Bannon

He's insane!

No, you're the crazy one!

My finger is on the button!

So is mine, and mine is bigger!

That was easy!

If only!

A exchange between Bannon and Trump. I wish I was making it up.

Asteroid of Awfulness!

Unknown to science, till now
Asteroids come in colors
The most recent one is orange
Because of its close approach
And its existential threat
They are calling it
The Asteroid of Awfulness!
The dinosaurs are waiting
To see what happens!

Speaking (01/14/18) on the BBC's Andrew Marr Show, Shadow First Secretary of State Emily Thornberry said President Donald Trump was a dangerous "asteroid of awfulness" and a "racist," after he reportedly referred to Haiti and a number of poor nations as "shithole countries."

"He is an asteroid of awfulness that has fallen on this world. I think that he is a danger, and I think that he is a racist," Thornberry said. "American democracy has a number of checks and balances, and I think there are a number of people who are important to speak to."

Are You a Nutjob?

The Wall

I never said Mexico
Will pay for the Wall
Never!
Trust me, never!
But a Wall is gooder
It is the best technology
The greatest!
It works!
Like the wheel
Old tech, best tech!
I'm a firm believer in tech.

My favorite movies are
Escape from New York
And, *Escape from L.A.*
They had great Walls!
Hell, the next movie should be:
Escape from the United States
Love it!

Look, China has the Great Wall
It's still there so I'm sure
That worked out just fine!
Then there was the Berlin Wall
And someone told me about
Hadrian's Wall
They keep building Walls
So they must be good
Right?

I never saw a Wall I didn't like!
Pink Floyd keeps singing about
Some damn Wall
See, must be good!
Trust me!
We need a Wall!
By the way, how long is
Our border with Canada?

Duty & History

Duty and history
Tell us what to do
Tell us why it should be done

Duty and history
Heavy burdens, indeed
Yet that is all we have
To guide us
Duty and history

They say that:
Only in death does duty end
But history can only show guideposts
Duty shows us challenges and purpose
It is our own will to choose
But duty and history demand a decision

Are You a Nutjob?

Toilets

There was a line to use the toilet
No problem, there was another one, free
There was this portly guy waiting
Waiting with a large toilet brush, held high
Living the dream? I joked,
To make conversation
Keeping in mind that men
Don't usually talk in public bathrooms
But, whatthehell, he looked so sad

What, he exploded, *I'm not a janitor!*
I'm the fuckin President of the United States!
This is my staff of office!
He said, brandishing his giant toilet brush

Sorry, I said, confused, *but what*
Are you doing in Barack Obama's
Presidential Library bathroom, then?
He looked lost and bewildered

I don't know, he stammered
One moment I was in the White House
Then I was here – but, I know stuff
That even the Generals don't!
But, I don't know how I got here!
He finished, plaintively

Perhaps it was something you said,
or, something you did?
I replied, still feeling sorry for
This portly, lost, caricature
Proudly displaying his new staff of office
Still, I offered some advice:
If you are going to be dealing in shit,
you might want to wear thick gloves!

Are You a Nutjob?

On December, 13, 2017, writing about President Trump's sexually suggestive statement that Sen. Kirsten Gillibrand (D-N.Y.) "would do anything" for campaign contributions, in an unusual editorial, USA Today declared that "a president who would all but call Sen. Kirsten Gillibrand a whore is not fit to clean the toilets in the Barack Obama Presidential Library or to shine the shoes of George W. Bush."

Are You a Nutjob?

38 Minutes at Mar-a-Lago

Terminator 2: Judgement Day
The Day the World Ended
By Dawn's Early Light
Fail-Safe
On the Beach
The Day After
Threads
WarGames -
Now, *38 Minutes at Mar-a-Lago*
Nuclear war imminent!
POTUS -
Too busy to respond?
Too lazy to respond?
Too ignorant to respond?
His staff too wise to tell him?
We are now entering the territory of
Dr. Strangelove!

On Saturday morning, January 13, 2018, a false ballistic missile alert was issued via the Emergency Alert System and Commercial Mobile Alert System over television, radio, and cellphones in the U.S. state of Hawaii. The alert stated that there was an incoming ballistic missile threat to Hawaii, advised residents to seek shelter, and concluded "This is not a drill". The message was sent at 8:07 a.m. local time. However, no civil defense outdoor warning sirens were authorized or sounded by the state. A second message, sent 38 minutes later, described the first as a "false alarm". Reportedly, Trump was playing golf at his resort, Mar-a-Lago, and did not respond for 38 minutes during which time the country was in a panic.

Sorry!

Sorry, I can't bake your cake
Sorry, you can't eat here
Sorry, I won't sell you my goods
Sorry, your child is now mine
Sorry, your voice sounds foreign
Sorry you are no longer my ally
Sorry I called you a little rocket man
Sorry I paid off a porn star
Sorry I hired illegal workers
Sorry I am destroying American institutions
Sorry I am ending world-wide
American respect
Sorry I colluded with anyone
Just anyone...
Sorry the White House is now really white
Sorry....Hell no, I'm not sorry!
But, I am really sorry for:
I'm sorry the fake media is out to get me!
I'm sorry the Left can't get over things!
I'm sorry you think kids are important!
I'm sorry I am the laughing stock
Of comedians all over the world!
I'm sorry my wife doesn't care!
I'm sorry the aliens came but
Weren't white Christians so they left!
I'm sorry about that damn Mueller!
Sorry....Where was I?

Are You a Nutjob?

Rape

(Later, not long after the crimes were committed,
A Senate Oversight Committee conducted
hearings to determine what, and how,
and why, the crisis happened in our country.
As part of the historical record the following
testimony was documented):

Senator Drew Fairchild (R) Alabama:
*To begin with, could you state your
name for the record?*

Witness: *My name is The Statue of Liberty.*

Senator Fairchild: *May I call you Ms. Liberty?
It is a 'Ms.' is that right?*

Witness: *Of course, senator. Yes it is.*

Senator Fairchild: *Now, Ms. Liberty, please
tell us in your own words, your version of
the events that unfolded and that you
were witnessed to.*

Witness: *I'd be pleased to senator. It is my
honor to address this august body....*

Senator Fairchild: *Ah, excuse me Ms. Liberty,
but do I detect a faint accent in your voice?*

Witness (a little perplexed): *Yes, senator, that
may be possible. I was not born in the United
States, but arrived here many years ago.*

Senator Fairchild: *Thank you for clearing that
up (whispering to an aide....inaudible).
Please continue.*

Are You a Nutjob?

Witness: *As I was saying, senator, with the advantage of my height, my advanced age and experience, combined with a clear view of the many comings and goings of Americans, I was able to see clearly what happened. I...*

Senator Fairchild: *Ah, again excuse me, Ms. Liberty, but I take it to mean that your so-called "clear view" means that you spend your time down by the harbor? Is that a yes or a no?*

Witness: *Ah, yes, senator, that is correct.*

Senator Fairchild: *Hmm, I thought so* (more whispering to an aide...inaudible). *Do you think the harbor is a safe place for a female, Ms. Liberty?*

Witness: *Apparently not, senator, as this is where I was repeatedly raped.*

(Roars from the chamber)

Senator Fairchild: *Quiet please. Quiet please, or I will clear the chamber! Now that is a serious charge, Ms. Liberty!*

Witness (very composed): *I realize that senator. But, I have ample witnesses and documented proof!*

Senator Fairchild: *Ah, Ms. Liberty, before we go into that - in closed session, may I ask you a question?*

Witness: *Of course, senator.*

Are You a Nutjob?

Senator Fairchild: *Ms. Liberty, on the occasion of these supposed rapes, what* (Senator Fairchild paused here), *what were you **wearing** down by that harbor you frequent?*

(Audible gasps for the audience, then a rising growl. At this point during the hearing, the Committee Chairman, Senator (R) Joshua White, requested a brief recess. The hearing never continued in open session. Historical note: A full record of the closed session was never revealed, despite repeated FOIA requests.)

Parade

As we got close to the reviewing stand
We all picked up our pace
Sharpening our strides
Our ranks turning their heads
In unison towards our great leader
Standing on the great stage
And we all executed a sharp salute
In the background the crowd cheering
Behind us, tanks rumbling
Heavy treads tearing up the street
Overhead, airplanes roaring past
Il Duce Supremo raising his arm in response
His famous orange hair
Like a wild tabby trying to escape
Blowing, waving in the god-wind
Created by the mass of arrayed troops
We are soldiers, we are an arm of the Republic
We all do our duty, fulfil our roles
But, never, never, have we felt so soiled!

The idea of a military parade, first promoted by Trump, was eventually cancelled..

Are You a Nutjob?

Independence Day

Fireworks exploding
Cheers and clapping
The gunpowder-scent of summer
Lingering in the humid air
And the rockets' red glare...
Sing it kids...!
*...your huddled masses yearning
to breathe free...*
No! No, not those lyrics!
It's the Fourth of July!
*...to live in a way that respects and
enhances the freedom of others.*
Stop it! Mandela, stop it!
It's the Fourth of July!
Barbecue with family later!
Great times!
*They who give up essential liberty
to obtain a little temporary freedom...*
Damnit Franklin, not now!
Wow! Look at that starburst!
Kids! Aren't we so damn lucky
To live in the land of the free....?
*Those who deny freedom to others
deserve it not for themselves.*
Oh, no, not you too, Lincoln!
Just leave me alone
I'm trying to enjoy Independence Day
With all my friends and family!
FREEDOM!
William Wallace, you stop it now!
Cover yourself!
Damnit, Honey, what was our
Congressman's number, again?
Can we now enjoy ourselves?
*I prefer liberty with danger than
peace with slavery.*
Okay, okay, Rousseau...

Are You a Nutjob?

All right, family, gather around
Hold hands and never let go!
And, remember, on this special day,
What Elie Wiesel once said:
Human suffering anywhere concerns
men and women everywhere.
Bang!
Now that was a firework!

I prefer liberty with danger than peace with slavery.
~ Jean-Jacques Rousseau

Those who deny freedom to others deserve it not for themselves.
~ Abraham Lincoln.

They who can give up essential liberty to obtain a little temporary
safety deserve neither liberty nor safety.
~ Benjamin Franklin

For to be free is not merely to cast off one's chains,
but to live in a way that respects and enhances the freedom of others.
~ Nelson Mandela.

Are You a Nutjob?

Seven Words

Little did we know that
George Carlin is actually alive!
Yes, alive!
Working incognito for the
U.S. government - but
They have tracked him down!
For now seven more words
Seven new words have been banned
From use in the government:
Vulnerable, entitlement, diversity,
Transgender, fetus, evidence-based,
Science-based – devil words!
Damn you, George!
You musta used them too much! -
Gotta be devil words!
Why else are they banned?
But, does that mean that those
Other, old, seven words can now
Be used without fear?
Shit, piss, fuck, cunt, cocksucker,
Motherfucker, and tits...
Wow! I said them!
The universe did not crack!
The sun still rises!
Lattes are still being served!
Can't wait to see those old seven words
Used in formal government reports, now!
Perhaps the Trump government
Actually knows what it is doing!
You think?
But, just in case
Run George, run, run...
The future may need you!!

Jim Crow

He left for awhile
No one thought he would
Ever come back
Lost at sea, some said
Others said he went abroad
But, no, some swear he was sighted
Sighted back in the South
No. He was sighted out West
New York....Chicago....St. Paul
He seemed to get around

Some claim to have seen
Strange fruit once again
Along with venom and violence
And separate but equal
And voter fraud
Can't be, can't be...
The KKK, Mr. Crow's friends
Want people back in their place
Tiki torches are in hot demand
No doubt to help them navigate
Back through a dark history

Mr. Crow, Mr. Crow,
Are you out there?
If so, here is one of your
Verses I particularly like
Before, before....

*...I'm for freedom,
An for Union altogether,
Although I'm a black man,
De white is call'd my broder.*

Make the Planet Great, Again!

Make the planet great, again!
Says France, with a straight face
Send us your tired, wretched scientists
Send us your poor, frustrated scientists
Send us all your scientists -
Huddled around that precious,
Fragile, flame of knowledge
Holding back the dark -
Yearning to breathe and speak freely
Send them, we welcome scientists
We believe in science
Viva la science!
And, as it doesn't seem like
You are still using the old lady
Can you consider sending back
The Statue of Liberty, too?

Amoral Familists

Amoral Familists
They look out for themselves
They look out for their own
Eventually it all spreads
Others follow their example
And society as a whole suffers
Especially when such a family
Is at the very top
To save society such families
Must be cut from the herd

BBC Mars

Good evening, this is BBC Mars
Conditions are worsening even more
Back on the home planet
A new round of wars has broken out
In the Middle East

Rising waters have wiped out
Even more island nations and coastal areas
The ozone hole has once again expanded
Due to lack of EPA enforcement
The sixth extinction is increasing
More rapidly than expected

While Mars has expanded its immigration
Policies and rates it is proving difficult
To fulfill our quotas due to the collapse
Of Earth space-faring nations

The Clarke Space Platform is reporting
The real-time collapse of both
The north and south ice sheets
Heinlein Moon Colony is reporting
A strong independence movement

Things look bad for Mother Earth
In other news, the Saturn Expedition....

Are You a Nutjob?

Lodestar

The snakes are everywhere, everywhere
I don't know where to put my feet
Or, my tiny, tiny hands
I'm scared to open drawers and cabinets
Papers are missing, things I left unsigned
Things I signed but can't find anymore
I don't know what I said last week
I did say something, right?
Doesn't matter, I'll just deny it
But, anyway, no worry
My lodestar, my trusty lodestar
Will point the true, true way

*The New York Times published a bombshell op-ed penned by an anonymous White House senior official on the intra-administration efforts to slam the brakes on President Trump's worst inclinations and ideas. The revelation of a resistance movement bubbling inside the West Wing opposing Trump on the basis of his "amorality" triggered a madcap race to identify the writer. "We may no longer have Senator [John] McCain," the writer opined. "But we will always have his example — a **lodestar** for restoring honor to public life and our national dialogue."*
"Lodestar" has never been identified.

Stoneman

Come on, guys
I'm sitting on all these stones
You used to love them, too!
Look they're everywhere
What do you need all
That metal shit for?
You have to dig it out
Of the ground, refine it,
Melt it, mold it-all kinds of work!
But, our stones, well, here
They just are - here like the
One I'm sitting on!
Come on, let's get back
To what made us great!
Let's get back to the Stone Age!

Most Dangerous?

ISIS
Al-Qaeda
The Taliban
The North Koreans
The Russians
The Chinese
Mexico
Immigrants
Shithole Countries
Democrats
Drugs
Organized crime
The Republican Party
Who is the most dangerous?
Most dangerous to America?
Most dangerous to the world?
Most dangerous to the planet?

Truth

Truth is a vast thing
Within this vastness
Lies, deceits, untruths
Fake truths
Are as nothing
Not even a dark candle
Sputtering in the light

Politicians

Politicians have such deft tongues
How is it then, that when they lick
The butts of the powerful
They cannot taste the shit?

Great People!

I am a bullet
Like most entities
I strive to live up to my potential
In fact, I hunger for it
A revolver is nice – for a slow day
An automatic handgun, even better
But neither lets me fully live up
To my full potential – Nope...
What I need to be fully alive
To be fully functional
To really fulfill my true purpose
Is an automatic rifle – fully automatic!
And, damn, if some people just
Don't do that for me!
They load me up and let me
Kill as many people as possible!
Such great people they are!
Great people!
How some can call them deranged
Call them mentally ill
Call them evil, is beyond me
They let me fulfill my destiny!
Great people, I tell ya!
Great people!
Please don't stop them!

Are You a Nutjob?

Booze, Women, & Movies

Booze, women, and movies
Wow! Such a good life!
I didn't know I had it so good!
But, I spent all my money
All my money on this!
No worries, I can get more
I'll just apply for more benefits!
Hell, I'll even get a third job!
Yes, I can do that
Who needs to sleep, after all?
Hell, the more I make
The more money I'll just spend on
Booze, women, and movies
But, dammit, I'm gonna squeeze
In a little latte, too...
I'll pretend I'm a rich politician!

On Nov, 29, 2017, Senator Chuck Grassley (R-Iowa), an ardent opponent of the estate tax, which, as part of the GOP's overall "Tax reform" package, will be eliminated, said in an interview: "I think not having the estate tax recognizes the people that are investing," Grassley said, "as opposed to those that are just spending every darn penny they have, whether it's on booze or women or movies."

How Soon?

How soon
Before they come for us?
Before they come for you and me?
How soon?
Immigrants, foreigners, different
All just ordinary folks
We see it already
Mass deportations
Random stops on trains and buses
Based on?

We see some resistance
We see some standing up
But, we see some embracing this
This New America
From powerful elite
To the person on the street
Will we all become *Good Germans*?
And just wait it all out
Hoping it will pass us by

After all, we obey the law
We are not *them*
Why would they come for us?
Marches, lawsuits, protests...
Will they be enough?
Were they enough before?

Choice & State

The separation of Choice and State.
The freedom to make a choice
Not one imposed by the State

Choice – such a big word
It implies freedom
Freedom of thought
Freedom of action
Freedom *from* imposed
Thought and actions
Where is the limit?
How much separation from
The State do we need/want?

Separation of Church and State
Freedom *of* religion as well as
Freedom *from* religion
Freedom to do as we please
Freedom from unwanted
Unwarranted rules, policies, laws
Freedom to kill and hunt
Till nothing is left?
Conservation?

Where is the limit?

Freedom to own weapons
Of our choosing
A pistol, a rifle, an automatic
A grenade launcher, a tank
A biological, a nuclear bomb?
Where is the limit?
Does the State have a role?
Any role?

Are You a Nutjob?

Policing – local, State, national?
National defense?
Interstate commerce?
International treaties?
Wherever the agreement is
It all depends on choice

Pro-life - pro-choice?
Apparently two polar opposites
Really?
Both sides want a choice
Their own choice
Not one imposed by another
Whatever their motivations and intentions
Gun control?
Both sides want a choice
Their own choice
Free Trade - Protectionism?
All sides want a choice
Their own choice

So many choices, so many options
Progressives – Conservatives?
Both sides want a choice
So, if *choice* is the common denominator
For all sides, for everyone
Why would anyone try to limit
Or impose their choice on someone else?

Why?
Mistrust?
Fear?
Hate?
Misunderstanding?

Are You a Nutjob?

Whatever the reason
If we all want *choice*
With a capital "C"
Then we must respect the power
And freedom of individual choice
Let others be wrong
Let others go to Hell
Let others live their lives
Where is the limit?
Where is *your* limit?

The separation of Choice and State
The fundamental premise
And promise of our nation -
And apparently, question
Choice and State
Where is the limit?

Concubine of Truth

Time is totally honest
It is the concubine of truth
It waits out all lies, all deceits
It pares away all defects
What is left cannot be argued with
Say what you will
You will soon be dead, anyway
Face time and say your piece

Good-News Story

Help...
Help us
Begs an island on its knees
We are dying here!

Trump's response:
Poor leadership in Puerto Rico
Not to listen and try harder
They want everything done for them...
He says from a luxury golf course
While he holds the power to help

In fact, Trump's Homeland Security
Calls this a *good-news story*
But, Puerto Rico calls this a
People-are-dying story

What do you call it?

Predator

Predator, remember the movie?
I especially liked: *Alien vs Predator*
But, now, the stakes are even higher
It is *Predator vs The American People!*

The Aliens are already on the run
The Predators appear to be winning
Hell, one is running on this very status:
Hey, look at me, I'm a Predator – Vote for me!

Running for the United States Senate!
No stealth technology here!
But, one of his brethren already beat
Him to it, and occupies the White House!

Still, no stealth tech there, either!
But, keep in mind that *Predators*
Are also *Alien* – in so many ways!

The Summit

The Summit of Summits

Are you a traitor Mr. President?
No, I am not! He replied
Standing next to Mr. Putin

Mr. Putin, is President Trump
a traitor to his country?
Yes he is! Replied President Putin
I wanted him to win the 2016 election
and I interfered in the election.

Mr. Trump, what do you say to that?

Well, Mr. Putin gave a strong and
powerful presentation. I think that
there is lots of blame to go around.

And, I've got to say, where,
where is the server, yes, where
is the server?

Troops to the Border!

Ho! Ho! Troops to the border!
Troops to the border!
Man the barricades!
Man the barricades!

Sir, we been here years now
And haven't seen any invaders

Oh, that's because they know
That we are here manning
These expensive barricades!

So, if they are not coming
Can we all go home now?

No! Hell no! That's just
What they are waiting for
So, instead, about-face troopers
We can't let anyone escape!

What to Do?

They walk among us
The stupid, the strange,
The deranged, the mentally ill,
The willfully ignorant
All undiagnosed
But still, they operate
Within our society
Unscathed, usually unnoticed
Somehow they function

Before it would be hidden
But today, with all the
Social media around us
They seem to be everywhere
They also seem to think that
Their ignorant opinions are
Of equal value and worth
To those of known scientists
And proven, hardcore facts

They tend to give Democracy
A bad name
But, what to do?

Women's March

Women march and march
All over the country
They march and march
Chanting his name
The Donald is pleased
He always knew women adored him!

Are You a Nutjob?

NEWS! NEWS! NEWS!

NEWS! NEWS! NEWS!
The Tomb of the Unknown Soldier
Has been moved!

For some reason that hasn't
Been fully explained
It has been moved to a sunny golf course!

Really…

To further clarify, White House
Spokesperson, Sara Muckelbie
Stated with a straight face
That the family of the Unknown Soldier
Filed a complaint about all the rain
Falling on their son's/daughter's Tomb

She added that she prays
This move would allow more people
To visit the Tomb
Particularly, those sun-loving,
God-fearing older Americans
That also love to golf

An efficient use of government
And tax payers' resources
She finished saying -
To an empty room
As no reporters were allowed
White House access

Making Sense?

Making sense?
How can we make sense
Of some things?
Umpqua, Sandy Hook,
Cologne, Virginia Tech,
Dunblane, Columbine,
Bath School,
Red Lake High School
Orlando, Las Vegas,
Stoneman,
Aurora
A fraternity of tragedy
The list can go on
And on...
A testament to what?

How evil we are?
How helpless we are?
How stupid we are?
Logic and reason fail
Faith takes a severe beating
We look to others
Authorities, experts
People of education
And influence
But nothing satisfies

No answer is good enough
How can such things happen?
How can people treat
Other people like that,
Especially children?

Are You a Nutjob?

Mental illness and evil
Have always been with us
But some things...
Some things just
Strike to the heart!

What kind of America
Do we have?
What type of America
Do we want?
What type of America
Do YOU want?

I would prefer to never update this poem again.

Climate Change

Climate change
Nope, not happening
Climate change
Trust me, I know
Climate change
Just a hoax
Climate change
Look at those really cold winters
Climate change
What climate change?
The Five Elements
Climate change
Anthropocene
What the hell is that?!
Climate change

Voice of America!

I need my own news service
One that will tell the truth
To America and the world
Report how great I am!
What a great job I am doing!
I know
I'll call it:
Voice of America!
Yeah, great
Voice of America!

What do you mean
That name has been taken?
I'm the real voice of America
Who else knows the truth
Like I do? Who else?
Voice of America!
I love it!

Hell, maybe:
Voice of Great America!
Yup, love it better…more words!
Confusion with an amusement park?
Nuts!

Who could make that mistake?!
Voice of Great America!
Love it!

Mr. Cohen

Mr. Cohen,
Do you swear to tell the truth
the whole truth and nothing but
the truth, so help you God?

Well, Sir, I don't know about God,
but I swear to tell the truth, this time

Republicans: *Tell us, Sir, why should*
we believe a lying scumbag like you?

Democrats: *Tell us, Sir, tell us about*
your relationship with Donald Trump
and what services you performed for him?

Mr. Cohen: *Well, I am a changed man,*
and have learned my lessons well,
and will have to live with what I have done,
which I deeply regret. I have also brought
documented evidence to back up
what I am saying.

Republicans: *Tell us, Sir, why we should*
we believe a lying scumbag like you?

Democrats: *Tell us, Sir, about*
your relationship with Donald Trump
and what services you performed for him?

Impeachment Party

I'm not interested in the Republican Party
Nor, the Democratic Party
Or, any Independent Party
The only party I'm interested in
He said, *is an Impeachment Party!*
He seemed quite irate
So, I didn't argue with him
And he also had me sign
My new book on Trump
Are You a Nutjob?
So, nothing like a satisfied customer!
Next, I called, hoping that in this crowd
No one was carrying

Summit Two

Presidential promises
I believe Mr. Kim
He didn't kill anyone!
So, we didn't make a deal
We took steps, though
Granted, very small steps
Doesn't matter that I lost
All my leverage
We're buddies
The art of the deal
That's me
Trust me

Are You a Nutjob?

Essays:

Some People

&

Are You a Nutjob?

Are You a Nutjob?

Are You a Nutjob?

We need a type of patriotism that recognizes the virtues of those who are opposed to us.
~ Francis John McConnell

The country is doing well in so many ways. But there's such divisiveness.
~ Donald J. Trump

It's hard to win an argument with a smart person, but it's damn near impossible to win an argument with a stupid person.
~ Bill Murray

You know, I was dealt a lot of bad hands.
~ Donald J. Trump

Don't take advice from an idiot, a moron, or a douche bag.
~ Amy Chow

When America retreats, chaos follows. When America Tweets, chaos follows.
~ Jamie el Bueno

Reductio ad Hitlerum *is not always wrong.*
- Thomas Banneker

A country cannot subsist well without liberty, nor liberty without virtue.
~ Daniel Webster

In a war of ideas it is people who get killed.
~ Stanisław Jerzy Lec

Are You a Nutjob?

Some People

Some people seem to have a certain mind(set) that appears to be immune to clear, deep, rational thought and reason. Their critical thinking faculty looks to be lacking, exampled by their very public embrace of implausible beliefs creating a context of credulity, where they accept, unchallenged, direct statements of *fact* easily refuted with a little research or open questioning.

They appear particularly to be affected and attracted to dogma, while professing to the myth of the stalwart individual, even while suborning their very own independence to any charismatic leader that may come along and appeal to their base fears and prejudices, easily bypassing the very rationality that they so strongly insist that they have in abundance.

They also seem to lack a certain curiosity about the universe in which we all live, beyond a certain utilitarian viewpoint that allows them to function, sometimes even thrive, in their own day-to-day world.

They can live in their air-conditioned homes, drive a modern vehicle, utilize a computer and smart phone, even insist on high-tech personal weapons, yet decry the very science that provides all these science-based tools and luxuries.

Formal education does not seem to affect or even penetrate this mind(set). Perhaps there is a genetic component, combined with a certain upbringing. It is difficult to know with any certainty.

They seem to think and reach decisions by exception, unable or unwilling to understand or appreciate any underlying principles that can either support or undermine their various positions.

Such people seem to be becoming more and more vocal, more obvious today. Their very willingness to throw away the very principles upon which this nation was founded and built is difficult to understand, except perhaps through the lens of some kind of failure in both nature and nurture.

However, it is certainly clear that when the psychopathology of the fundamentalist or opportunist, of whatever stripe, remains uncontested, bad things will follow.

They muddy the water, to make it seem deep.
~ Friedrich Nietzsche

Are You a Nutjob?

Are You a Nutjob?

Not that long ago nutjobs used to hide the fact that they were nutjobs; or, at least, they would be uncomfortable, even embarrassed, expressing nutjob views, hiding them from public view, perhaps only expressing them in their own nutjob churches, nutjob societies, and other nutjob organizations, or, just hiding them in their own nutjob skulls.

But, now, under the guise of political correctness, diversity, or, some supposed, perverse humanism, we have somehow given the nutjobs free reign. It's like getting social promotions in school – everyone is a winner! Every opinion has weight. But that's not true. Everyone is not a winner. Not all the time. Not all opinions are equal. Some are just plain wrong and stupid! In this case, a nutjob is a nutjob is a nutjob; and, if not for their own good, then certainly for our good, they should be told so and held accountable for their nutjob views and what they are doing to us and society in general.

If nutjobs cannot look at information, process data, absorb an education, and use the hardwiring of their brains to understand the world and the universe as it is, not as they may want it to be, then that is on them. The rest of us are not responsible for their nutjob views, nor should we tolerate them any more than we would someone who is mentally ill telling us how the world is and how it should be run. For make no mistake, it is a type of mental illness! One day it will be listed in the DSM (Diagnostic and Statistical Manual of

Mental Disorders) under Nutjob, perhaps as a Personality Disorder, certainly an Adjustment Disorder!

So, while we may feel sorry for them and try to do our best for them, we cannot allow their nutjob views to influence us in the real world and determine our fate.

Of course, we have to ask ourselves how do we establish who the nutjobs are and what is a nutjob view-point? You could say that it is a lot like pornography, we know it when we see it – but, is this true, and is it always true?

Perhaps some general guidelines would help:

- Does a view-point ignore current scientific evidence? (Sidebar: Yes, science is sometimes wrong. Yes, science is incomplete. Yes, science was created by fallible humans. All true. The big difference here between science and nutjob views is that science knows these things. Science at its core is about destroying itself and then re-creating itself, again and again...and again).

- Does a view-point hold back information and knowledge to the betterment of a few and to the detriment of the many?

- Is a view-point rational; that is, rational in the sense that it can hold up to open and clear scrutiny? If not.....

- Is a view-point based on dogma or data? Does dogmatic belief replace rational discourse and available evidence?

Are You a Nutjob?

- Is a view-point's purpose to hurt others? That is, does this view-point have as its aim to denigrate other people and their position in the world? To create the *Other* as the enemy, sometimes to the point of actually physically hurting or killing other people, just because they may disagree with you or hold a different belief system.

- Is a view-point arbitrarily binary – that is, are you with us or against us, based on nothing more than a difference in belief or opinion?

Anyway, I think you can see what I am thinking and saying. So, the big question is: Are you a nutjob? Stay calm, of course you aren't. That other guy is, not you! So, stand up and present and justify your view-point!

Ah, but here's the rub. The nutjob will not listen, or, perhaps even process, a rational, logical, data supported discussion. So, you have seen the above guidelines. If someone can't or won't follow them, it is your duty to stand up and say so. Say: *You are a nutjob. You have a right to your view* (remember, a nutjob would not allow you that same right!), *but you do not have the right to inflict your nutjob view on me and others. So, go back to your cave and let the rest of us go boldly, and fallibly, into the future! Ad Astra, please!*

Too much to ask? Yes, for nutjobs it is (another sign that they are nutjobs - their degree of intolerance is intolerable). The only remedy I can offer is to constantly and bravely stand up to nutjobs. Not that they will listen (another sign), but others may listen that are just confused or ignorant, and then may actually see the nutjobs for what they are. Overcoming nutjobs; only then can we really call ourselves a modern, rational, humane society that can have a chance of surviving and prospering, not only as a civilization, but as a species. Yes, the risks and costs are that dire. Have no illusion, make no mistake; while some nutjobs are basically harmless, others are crazy enough to endanger all of us, and, perhaps, the planet itself.

I am reminded of what the late Carl Sagan said: *We live in a society exquisitely dependent on science and technology, in which hardly anyone knows anything about science and technology.* This seems to lead inexorably to something that the late Arthur C. Clarke also said: *Any sufficiently advanced technology is indistinguishable from magic.*

For many people in today's world the technology that they use on a daily basis, and upon which they are so exquisitely dependent, is a total black box. From their air-conditioned, centrally-heated homes, to their modern cars, their TVs, computers, and smart phones, all of it, may just as well be magic, for all their understanding. Of course, no one today can be expected to fully understand everything in the world and how everything works, but the general principles should be known and understood. That it is not magic! It is science and that this science is based upon certain knowledge, principles and processes.

I should point out here that having education and standing in the sciences does not make anyone exempt from being a nutjob or holding nutjob views. We don't have to look far to see this is true. So, we just have to look at our established guidelines to help us in our decision making process as to whether or not someone is a nutjob, regardless of any scientific or educational credentials that person may have.

Are You a Nutjob?

So, when a nutjob stands up and declares some nutjob view-point, people should be able to place this view-point in the continuum of current scientific or common knowledge, or at least, know how to research and find out where this view-point stands on this continuum. And be able to ask how likely is this view-point to be true or accurate based on currently accepted scientific or common knowledge? This doesn't mean that some far-out view-point or theory may not be true, just how *likely* is it to be true based on what we currently know and understand? You can't just throw out a thousand or more years of scientific, rational, and humanistic thought and struggle just because some idea or belief sounds lovely today – oh, but I forgot, if you are a nutjob, yes you can! It is part of their psychopathology, after all.

I shave with Occam's razor and try to follow The Law of Parsimony, as needed. Can any view-point or theory stand up to these simple rules and their scrutiny? Is this review, critical thinking process perhaps too difficult a task for most of us?

Who knows? But, it's your choice. Your decision. What are you going to do?

But, to scarily quote Clarke again: *It has yet to be proven that intelligence has any survival value.*

As I understand it, the four major drivers of Civilization are: war, trade, religion, and climate change.

We all, as rational human beings, have a say in all of these four drivers. But, to make this say worthwhile and constructive, we need the best from all of us.

So, who owns the future? You or the nutjobs!?

Are You a Nutjob?

The poem, *Who Owns the Future?*, summarizes this essay.

Who Owns the Future?

When critical thinking is lacking
And the public embrace of implausible beliefs
Creates a context of credulity
When the psychopathology
Of the fundamentalist remains unchallenged
When injustice becomes law
When simple truth is considered treason -
Or, heroism....or, even heretical
When people of good will
Keep quiet and stand aside
Then society is in trouble
Then, what is left?
What can be done?
Who will do it?

We can look at the past
We can look at the present
We can look at Authority
In all its guises
We can look deep within ourselves
Can we then see the future?
What do we see?
What do we want to see?
Each of us must do their part
Each of us, every day, must stand up
Stand up and say *No!*
No, not here! No, not now! No, not ever!
This is when defiance becomes duty!
And civil disobedience becomes a responsibility
If not an obligation!
This is when we determine
Who owns the future

Are You a Nutjob?

When this essay was first published elsewhere, the following question came up. My answer follows.

Why do you blame diversity *and* political correctness *for the proliferation of nutjobs?*

The proliferation of nutjobs has come about via various and numerous means. I mentioned the two above and associated them with social promotions in the school system because they are sometimes used as umbrella excuses for not telling someone that they are nutjobs. Under *diversity* we have to allow everyone under the tent, even those bent on destroying the tent. Under *political correctness* we refrain from telling someone that they are nutjobs because, ah, that just wouldn't be nice. Everyone, after all, is entitled to their opinion, as crazy as they are. Entitled to these crazy opinions they may be, but we should not be constrained in calling a duck a duck (or, in this case, a nutjob a nutjob).

As has been pointed out, the media has recently given nutjobs a megaphone with which to announce their nutjobiness. Perhaps this explains the seeming proliferation of nutjobs today. In the past, view-points, opinions, theories used to go thru some kind of societal filtering process, filtering thru the rocks, gravel, and sand of the various strata of society, and Darwinian-like, surviving or not. Now with the rise and explosion of social media, nutjobs can by-pass this filtering process and give vent to their nuttiness unfiltered.

The tipping point for me was a recent election somewhere out west where a candidate won a primary (I won't mention the Party), by a hefty margin, according to the news reports, despite her publicly stating that tornadoes and the increased severe weather is caused by God's punishment for humans allowing gay marriage and equal rights. Regardless of how we may feel about this issue, this is nutjobiness personified! Yet, this person is running for high public office and, worse yet, other people are voting for her!

So, I sat down the next day and wrote this down just to get my frustration out of my system.

Keep in mind that all this happened before the current President entered office. Now things have just escalated, bringing out, even more, those who have a nutjob view-point and agenda. I would also note that this nutjob trend appears to operate outside the United States, as well.

The world is in a state of flux, probably exacerbated by climate change. It is at this point we all need clarity and good rational judgement the most. Simple fixes for all the complex problems we all face are an illusion. The only walls we really need are those that protect us all against the approaching darkness.

Are You a Nutjob?

Are You a Nutjob?

True freedom comes from the ground up, it is not bequeathed from above. If it is, then by that very premise, it can also be taken away.

~ James Darwin

Are You a Nutjob?

Are you a Nutjob?

Are you a Nutjob?